Being the **Best Me!**

Feel Confident!
A book about self-esteem

Cheri J. Meiners

★

illustrated by Elizabeth Allen

free spirit
PUBLISHING®

Text copyright © 2013 by Cheri J. Meiners, M.Ed.
Illustrations copyright © 2013 by Free Spirit Publishing Inc.

Library of Congress Cataloging-in-Publication Data
Meiners, Cheri J., 1957–
      Feel confident! / Cheri J. Meiners, M.Ed. ; illustrated by Elizabeth Allen.
            pages cm. — (Being the best me)
      Audience: Age 4–8.
      ISBN-13: 978-1-57542-442-2 (paperback)
      ISBN-10: 1-57542-442-8 (paperback)
      ISBN-13: 978-1-57542-453-8 (hardcover)
      ISBN-10: 1-57542-453-3 (hardcover)
1. Self-confidence in children—Juvenile literature. I. Allen, Elizabeth (Artist) illustrator. II. Title.
      BF575.S39M45 2013
      155.4'191—dc23
                                                            2013011667

ISBN: 978-1-57542-442-2

Free Spirit Publishing does not have control over or assume responsibility for author or third-party websites and their content.

Reading Level Grade 1; Interest Level Ages 4–8;
Fountas & Pinnell Guided Reading Level H

Cover and interior design by Tasha Kenyon
Edited by Marjorie Lisovskis

10 9 8 7 6 5
Printed in Hong Kong
P17200417

Free Spirit Publishing Inc.
6325 Sandburg Road, Suite 100
Minneapolis, MN 55427-3674
(612) 338-2068
help4kids@freespirit.com
www.freespirit.com

Free Spirit offers competitive pricing.
Contact edsales@freespirit.com for pricing information on multiple quantity purchases.

To my beautiful and accomplished daughter Julia:
May you always feel confident with who you are
and who you are becoming.

I like being me—
a very important person!

1

At every age, each person is important and has something to say.

I'm important to my family.
They know me best and love me.
I belong, and I feel needed.

5

I'm learning to take care of myself.

I like the way I look.
No one else looks just like me.

7

Each day I grow
and get stronger.

I love all that my body can do!

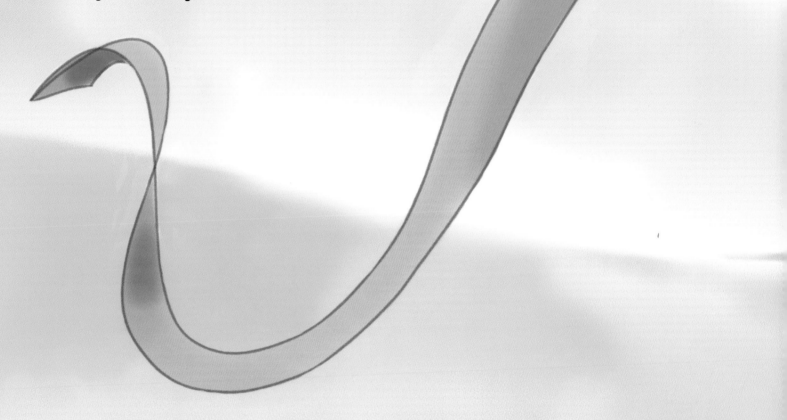

see

smell

hear

touch

breathe

sing

jump

run

dance

walk

9

My mind is strong, too.
I can choose to think confident thoughts.

I am the only person
just like me!
I can accept myself
just the way I am.

I can try lots of new things.

I might like them
and be good at them.

I show that I believe in myself when I stand up straight, look people in the eye, and smile.

I can say "thank you" when someone says something nice to me.

Thank you!

I'm able to think and decide for myself.

18

When I make good choices,
I can feel proud of myself.

Okay,
we'll watch
your show.

When there is a problem,
I can try to do something about it,

or ask for help.

21

I believe that I can do hard things.

When I do my best and keep trying,
I get better at being me.

23

I'm able to speak up
and tell people how I feel
and what I want.

24

When I feel good about myself,
it's easy to see good in others, too.
I like myself when I'm kind.

27

I am important,
and I'm able to do
important things.

28

I can believe in myself
and all that I have to give.

I feel confident that I can be
the person I want to be—

because in many ways I already am.

Ways to Reinforce the Ideas in *Feel Confident!*

Feel Confident! teaches confidence and self-esteem—an outlook on one's life that reflects what a person *is* (one's inherent importance or worth), and what one *does* (including a belief that one is *able* to learn and achieve). A realistic and healthy sense of self can lead to improved mental and physical health, better school performance, greater feelings of fulfillment, improved relationships, and a greater sense of control over one's life—all of which lead to greater happiness. Children's confidence can increase as they become more aware of their own unique identity and attributes, and as they incorporate principles learned in the book. In addition, the activities on pages 33–35 can encourage children's appreciation of both their worth and their abilities and can assist in developing skills that nurture children's self-esteem. Here is a quick summary of confidence skills, most of which are mentioned in the children's text:

1. Take care of yourself.
2. Be happy with how you look.
3. Focus on things you do well.
4. Make decisions for yourself.
5. Face challenges and try to solve them.
6. Keep trying when things are hard.
7. Speak up for your needs.
8. Compliment others.
9. Be kind and treat others with respect.
10. Expect things to work out.

Words to know:

Here are terms you may want to discuss:

able: having the power to do something

accept: to feel that you belong and are okay just the way you are

belong: to be an important part of a group of people, like a family

confident: believing in oneself; feeling strong, sure, and trusting

imagine: to have a picture in your mind about something

trust: to believe that something is true

As you read each spread, ask children:

- What is happening in this picture?
- What is the main idea?
- How would you feel if you were this person?

Here are additional questions you might discuss:

Pages 1–7

- What does your family say you were like as a baby? Why do you think you are special to your family? (*Help children see that being who they are makes them special, apart from anything they might be particularly good at.*)

- What does it mean to be important? (*It means that people care about you, and you matter to them.*)

- What does it mean that each person "has something to say"? (*We all have feelings, ideas, and things we like that matter to us and to someone else.*) What do you think are things that young children have to say? (*Babies and young children have things to say like, "I want to be held" or "I'm happy."*) How might a person "say" things without talking? (*People can share the things they feel and think about without using words. They can use their hands, their bodies, or sounds to "say" things, too.*)

- What does your name mean? How do you feel when someone knows your name and uses it?

- What is something special about your family?

- What does it mean to belong? What do people in your family need you for?

- What is something you like about the way you look?

Pages 8–17

- What things have you learned to do to feel strong and happy? What do you do to take care of yourself? How often do you do these things?

- What are some things you can do for yourself? What can you do now that you couldn't do when you were younger?

- Is there something about yourself or your life that you wish you could change? Why is it helpful to accept things that you can't change?

- What does it mean to look someone in the eye? When you stand straight and look people in the eye, how do you feel? How do you think other people feel when you smile and look them in the eye?

Pages 18–31

- What is something you can decide for yourself? How do you feel when you do what you think is best?

- Can you think of a problem you were able to solve by yourself? When was a time you needed help? Who are some grown-ups you can talk to when you need help?

- Did you ever do something hard? How did it feel to do that? Did you have to try more than one time? How did it feel to keep trying? Did you feel more confident after doing it?

- When has it been hard for you to speak up and say how you feel? What could you say the next time?

- When is a time you told someone how you feel, or what you want? Do you think you were kind? How did it turn out?

- Tell about a time when you complimented (*said something nice to*) someone. What did the person do or say? Did that make you feel more confident? If yes, why do you think so? If no, why not?

- What are some important things you can do?

- What makes you feel confident about yourself?

Games and Activities for Feeling Confident

Read this book often with your child or group of children. Once children are familiar with the book, refer to it when teachable moments arise, both those involving healthy self-esteem and those relating to low self-esteem or discouragement. In addition, use the following activities to reinforce children's understanding of self-esteem and self-confidence.

Name That Important Person

Preparation: Send home a note to families asking them to discuss with the child the significance of the child's name and why the child received it.

Materials: Large index cards for name tags; hole punch and yarn; crayons or markers

Directions: Have each child make and decorate a name tag. Help children punch holes and thread and tie yarn so they can hang the name tags around their neck. While wearing their name tags, children can tell the group how and why they received their name or what makes their name special.

Children might share their name's origin and original meaning, if known; who or what they were named after; or why their parents thought the name was special or important. If a child does not know any background about his or her name, ask what the name means to the child and what the child especially likes or appreciates about it.

"All About Me" Scrapbook

Materials: Slips of paper, small container or paper bag to hold the slips of paper; a notebook (Level 1) or three-ring binder and hole-punched paper (Level 2) for each child; pencils, crayons, markers

Preparation: Write several questions on the slips of paper. (Examples: "Where were you born?" "What is your favorite color/dessert/sport?" "Who is in your family?" "What is a game you like to play?") Fold and put the slips in a small container or paper bag. Children will draw one question each day.

Level 1

In their notebooks, have children draw, write, or dictate a response to the question of the day. Afterward, invite children to discuss their responses with the group. As a variation, you might read some responses and ask children to guess who wrote them.

Level 2

As an ongoing project, have each child continue to add to the scrapbook binder examples of special work, drawings, photos, and memorabilia that represent things the child likes and participates in. The child can write or dictate captions explaining the significance of each page.

"I Can Do That" Bingo Game

Materials: 3" x 5" index cards; paper and pen or marker; tokens such as pennies, paper clips, or buttons; small plastic bags or paper cups for each child to hold tokens

Preparation: Prepare bingo cards by making a grid of 1" squares with 3 to 5 rows across and 3 to 5 squares in each row. Print a copy of the grid for each child. Make "I Can Do That" cards by writing a skill on each index card. Include developmentally appropriate activities that children are able to do, such as the following: *get dressed, wash hands, dust, eat with a fork, read, ride a bike or trike, draw, count to 10, sing a song, throw a ball, write my name, make a sandwich, brush my teeth.* Decide on a simple symbol for each skill and draw it on the card. *(Example: For "Eat with a fork," draw a simple fork.)*

First Time Only

As you read each card aloud, have children draw the symbol in a random box of their grid. When grids have a symbol in each square, you may wish to preserve the bingo boards by laminating them or placing them in a plastic sleeve.

Level 1

Play bingo. As you or a child draws a card and names an activity, children will cover the corresponding square on their card with a token if they "can do that." When a child covers a row in any direction, the child calls "Bingo!" and the round ends.

Level 2

The child who finished first can act out one of the skills on the card while other children guess what the child is role-playing.

"Journey of Confidence" Virtual Vacation

Preparation: Gather several slides or online photos that depict various interesting activities and places. Your photos might include exotic locales (the jungle, a faraway desert, a big amusement park, a bazaar full of stalls with street food) and daring activities (swinging from branches, riding a camel, flying in a hot-air balloon, trying new foods). Organize them as a slideshow of a make-believe trip. Be prepared to display the photos on a screen or whiteboard.

Directions: Introduce the activity by telling children you are going on a "trip" together. You might start with everyone sitting and riding in the "airplane" to your destination; you could narrate the take-off, the sights below as the plane rises, and the landing. Then ask children to stand as you "arrive" at your destination and begin your virtual adventures. Narrate the sights, the sounds, and the activities they are participating in as they view the photographs. Explain any aspects that might seem difficult, hard, or new to a child. For example, you might say: "We have a chance to go deep-sea diving and look at these bright blue fish up close! We'll have to wear a wet suit and flippers, and a tank for breathing. Let's get ready! Is everybody coming along on our dive?"

If there is something children wouldn't want to actually do, explain that they may sit down and leave the trip if they like, but that they will not be able to stand up and rejoin the trip later. Allow time at various moments in the "trip" for children to decide about this. The point is not to be rigid or punitive but to help children recognize that choosing not to try new things can mean they will not enjoy experiences fully. After your short "trip," have all the children sit down.

Discussion: Ask children if they enjoyed the trip. For children who sat down and "left the trip" at some point, ask if something happened later in the trip that they wished they could stand up and do. Explain that this can happen in real life, too. If we decide not to try things, we might miss out on many fun or exciting experiences. For example, someone who decides not to try to ride a bike won't be able to ride to the park or to a ball field with other kids or with the family. When we are confident in ourselves, we will feel more willing to try new things. We will get to do a lot of things we may like, and we will keep feeling even more confident.

Child of the Day

Directions: Make a rotating schedule to allow each child an opportunity to be special for the day. You may decide to incorporate this into your daily schedule, allowing each child various opportunities—such as being a leader, being first in line, or passing out materials; bringing an item from home or sharing an experience with the class; doing an errand for the teacher; or spotlighting the child's responses in the "All About Me" scrapbook discussions.

Picture of Confidence

Materials: Magazines, scissors, large index cards, glue, drawing paper, crayons and markers, glue sticks

Preparation: Cut pictures from magazines of people confidently doing various activities (such as shooting a basketball, cooking, raising a hand to answer a question, dancing, making a repair, helping someone else). If desired, glue the pictures to large index cards.

Level 1
Explain that a person who is confident feels *important* and *able* to do things. Show magazine pictures to children one at a time. Ask "Does this person seem confident? Why do you think so?"

Level 2
Prompt children to discuss situations in which they feel *important* and *able*. Have children make a collage by drawing or cutting and pasting words and pictures of things they like about themselves, things they like and are able to do, as well as things they would like to learn to do.

Confident Me

Materials: Large index cards and marker; whiteboard; writing paper and pencil for each child (for Extension)

Directions: Explain that the group will name some positive (good) things about each other. Invite one child to stand up, and ask the other children to name a positive characteristic about that child. You might prompt the discussion with a question that includes examples, such as: "What is something positive about Jeremy? Is he kind? Does he make you feel happy when he laughs?" Invite several responses. Write the traits discussed on the whiteboard and also on an index card that the child can keep. (If you wish, write the traits on the back of the child's name tag from the "Name That Important Person" activity on page 33.) Continue, identifying positive traits for each child in your group.

Extension: Review the traits written on the whiteboard. Ask children to choose three positive words that they feel describe themselves. Also write these on the child's index card (or the back of the name tag). Then have children write or dictate to you a few sentences about themselves using the positive words they selected. Offer your own positive observations as well.

Get the Whole Being the Best Me! Series
by Cheri J. Meiners

Books that help young children develop character traits and attitudes that strengthen self-confidence, resilience, decision-making, and a sense of purpose.
Each book: 40 pp., color illust., PB, 11¼" x 9¼", ages 4–8.

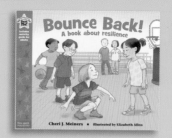

Learning to Get Along® Series Interactive Software

Free Spirit's Learning to Get Along® Series by Cheri J. Meiners

Help children learn, understand, and practice basic social and emotional skills. Real-life situations, diversity, and concrete examples make these read-aloud books appropriate for childcare settings, schools, and the home.
Each book: 40 pp., color illust., PB, 9" x 9", ages 4–8.